My name is Lucas.

What is your name? _____

I Can't Sit Still!
Living with ADHD

Pam Pollack & Meg Belviso
Illustrations: Marta Fàbrega

IMPOSSIBLE TO WAIT...

Today the teacher put a math problem on the board.
"Who knows the answer?"
Some kids raised their hands.
I shouted out, "Three!"

"We don't shout out answers," the teacher said.

"That is against the rules."

I have trouble following rules.

I looked out the window. I wished it were time for recess.

The teacher called my name. "You're not paying attention," she said.

I have trouble paying attention too.

TO PAY ATTENTION

THE RULES AGAIN

I was so happy to go out on the
playground for recess. It's hard for me
to sit still at my desk. Some kids were
playing kickball. I ran to first base.
"You can't run to first base until you
kick the ball," my friend said.
"And you have to wait your turn.
Those are the rules."
"I hate rules!" I shouted at my friend.
I kicked the fence hard.
"We don't want to play with you
anymore," my friend said.
"When you don't follow the rules,
you ruin the game."

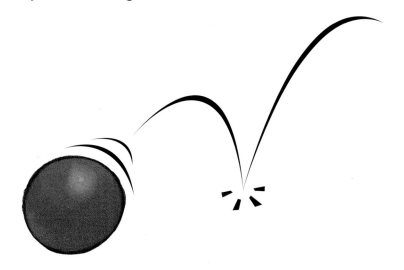

I TRY TO DO THINGS RIGHT!

When I got home I was still sad that
my friend was angry at me.
I went to my room. My mom was
there. "You forgot how to make your
bed this morning?" she asked.
"You pulled the covers up, but you left
your pillow on the floor."
"I didn't mean to forget!" I shouted.
"I tried to do it right!"
Mom didn't get mad. She said
it wasn't my fault.

Mom said I had something called
ADHD: Attention Deficit Hyperactivity
Disorder. I got a little scared, but Mom
told me I would be OK.
The next day my parents took me to see
a special doctor. "People with ADHD
can't wait their turn or follow rules," he
explained. "They forget to finish things."
"That's just like me!" I said.

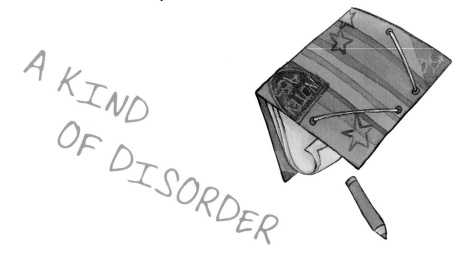

A KIND
OF DISORDER

WHAT A MESS OF MESSAGES!

"Imagine that your head is full of people who carry messages from one part of your brain to another," said the doctor. "ADHD makes it hard for them to do that. The messages get lost or can't get through. Like the message that reminds you to raise your hand before you speak in class. Or tells you all the steps you need to make your bed."

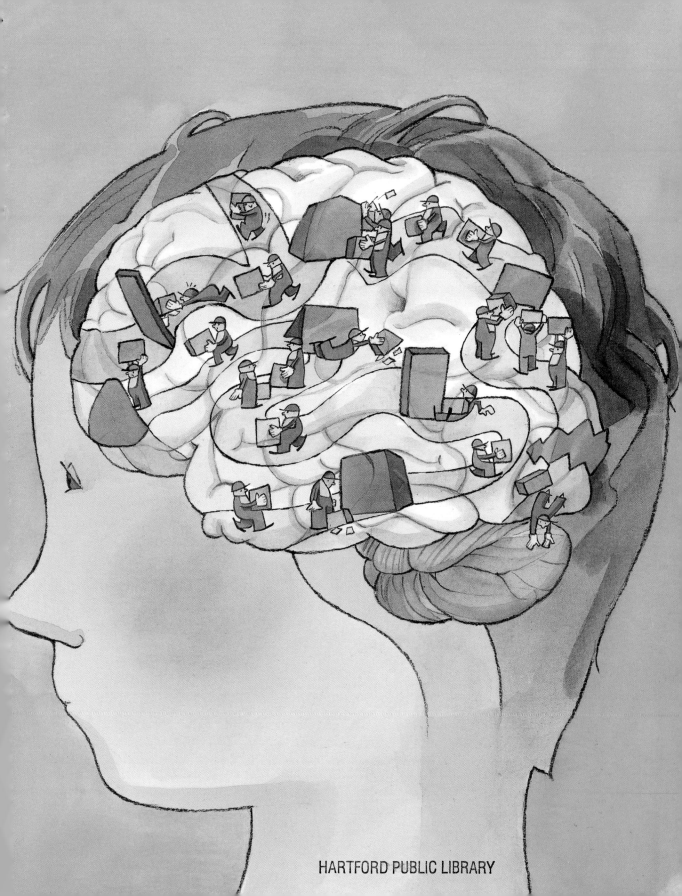

HARTFORD PUBLIC LIBRARY

MY SCHEDULE

The doctor gave me medicine to take once a day. The medicine would help my brain do its job. He helped my family make a schedule of everything I had to do during the day: Get up, have breakfast, make my bed, take my pill, go to school, play, do homework, eat dinner, go to bed. Everything went on my schedule.

The doctor showed me how to break things I had to do down into steps. That would help me finish them.

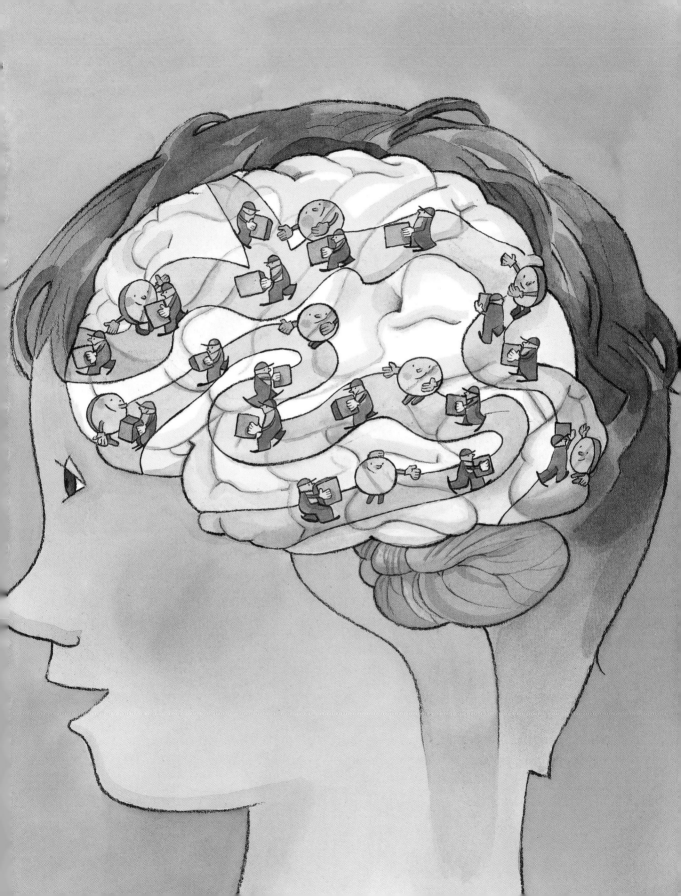

MOM IS HELPING ME

My Dad put the schedule on the wall at home. There was a note on it. It said that at four o'clock every day I had to play dolls with my little sister. I laughed because I realized she had written it.

I took off the note. "You are not allowed to write things on my schedule," I told her. "This is no fun for me," she said.

Mom and I cleaned my room and put everything in the right place. I used to lose my things all the time. Now I should always know where they are.

IMPROVING DAY BY DAY

It was a lot easier to remember everything when I followed my schedule.

First thing in the morning I got up. Then I followed all the steps to make my bed:

1. Smooth bedsheets.

2. Pull up bedspread.

3. Put pillows in their place.

"Good job," my Dad said. "You've made your bed every day this week and everything in your room is in its place. The doctor will be happy when we go to see him again."

1.

2.

3.

RULES AT SCHOOL

Things were better at school too.
My teacher knew about ADHD too. We made a deal.
She said if it got too hard for me to sit still in my seat,
I could walk quietly in the back of the room.
That helped. She also made me a list of classroom rules
that I used to forget. I keep the list at my desk.

IT BECOMES EASIER

My medicine made it easier
to pay attention and wait my turn.
When I knew the answer,
I remembered to raise my hand first.
"Very good," my teacher said.
"Now it's time for recess."

I CAN CONTROL MYSELF!

Some kids started up a kickball game.
"Do you want to play?" my friend asked.
I joined the team. I stood at the end
of the line to wait my turn to kick the ball.
There were three kids ahead of me.
I wanted to push to the front of the line.
But I didn't.

NOW IS MY TURN

It was my turn. I looked out at first base.
That's where I was supposed to go. But that
wasn't following the rules.

1. I waited until the pitcher rolled the ball to me.

2. I kicked the ball.

3. I ran to first base. My team cheered.

WHAT A NICE TEAM!

Because of my kick my team scored two more points.
We won the game!
"It's awesome to have you on our team," my friend said.
I was glad to have my doctor, my teacher, and my family
on *my* team. ADHD means some things are harder for me.
But it doesn't mean I can't have fun!

Activities

WHAT'S
MISSING?

Kids with ADHD sometimes have trouble focusing. This game will improve your concentration and your memory.

What you need: two or more people and a table.

Player 1 arranges some objects on a table. They can be any kind of objects at all and as many as you like. For instance: an orange, a key, a sneaker, a playing card, and a spoon.

Player 2 studies the table and leaves the room. Player 1 removes one object from the table. When Player 2 returns, he or she has to say what is missing. If the answer is wrong, Player 1 and any other players can ask Player 2 to do silly things, like singing and dancing, or pretending to be a chicken. Give one point for every successful answer, and add the points at the end of the game to see who's the winner. You may add more objects as you get better at it.

SIMON SAYS—WITH A TWIST

ADHD makes it hard to remember lots of instructions. This game will help you improve your memory.
What you need: Two or more people.
One person is Simon. Simon orders the other players to do something like "shake your head." Then Simon adds something else: "Shake your head and quack like a duck." Everyone does both things. See who can remember the most things at once.
To avoid confusion, Simon should prepare a list of orders before the game starts.
When you have a winner, that person gets to be Simon in the next round.

SEVEN-MINUTE STORY

Choose three or four things to tell a story. For instance, a plastic dinosaur, a superhero action figure, a stuffed dog. Give yourself seven minutes to make up a story using those three things. The story has to have a beginning, something exciting, and an end.

If you are alone, you can tell the story to yourself. If you are with friends, you can have a contest: who tells the best story?

Parent's guide

T he behavioral disorder called ADHD affects 4% to 12% of school-age children. It is more common in boys.

Does your child have ADHD?
An inattentive child with ADHD will have six or more of the following symptoms:
• Finds it hard to follow instructions
• Has trouble paying attention at school, home or while playing sports
• Loses things at school and at home
• Does not seem to listen
• Is careless about details
• Is disorganized
• Has trouble planning ahead
• Forgets things
• Is easily distracted

A hyperactive child with ADHD will have at least six of the following symptoms:
• Fidgets or squirms
• Can't play quietly
• Blurts out answers
• Interrupts
• Can't sit still
• Talks too much
• Has trouble waiting turns

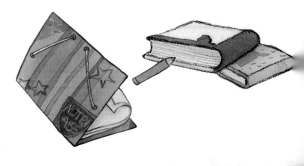

Will medicine or therapy cure ADHD?

There is no cure for ADHD. A combination of medications, such as Ritalin, and behavioral therapy can help increase attention span and decrease impulsiveness. Obviously, the drug treatment and the behavioral therapy must be directed by a qualified physician.

How can I help my child?

The best thing you can do at home for a child with ADHD is to provide structure and routine.

- Make a schedule. Explain any changes to the routine in advance.
- Make clear house rules. Explain and write down what will happen when the rules are obeyed and when they are broken.
- Keep directions simple and short and repeat them if necessary. Ask your child to repeat the directions back to you to make sure they were heard and understood.
- Congratulate your child when he or she completes each step of a task.
- Limit playtime to one or two friends at a time.
- Set a homework routine with regular breaks. Check homework to make sure it has been completed.
- Reward your child for good effort, not grades.

Parenting a child with ADHD has its challenges, but ADHD children have a special way of seeing the world and you can share it with them. Always remind yourself—and your child—how great he or she is.

ADHD does not keep a child from making friends, doing well in school and, most important, being happy. History is full of famous people who had ADHD, such as Olympic swimmer Michael Phelps, John F. Kennedy, and Albert Einstein. ADHD not only did not hold them back, it made them who they are.

I CAN'T SIT STILL! Living with ADHD

First edition for the United States and Canada
published in 2009 by
Barron's Educational Series, Inc.

© Copyright 2009 by Gemser Publications S.L.
El Castell, 38; Teià (08329) Barcelona, Spain
(World Rights)

Title of the original in Spanish:
¡No puedo estar quieto! Mi vida con ADHD

Author: Pam Pollack and Meg Belviso

Illustrator: Marta Fàbrega

*All inquiries should be
addressed to:*
Barron's Educational Series, Inc.
250 Wireless Boulevard
Hauppauge, NY 11788
www.barronseduc.com

ISBN-13: 978-0-7641-4419-6
ISBN-10: 0-7641-4419-7

Library of Congress
Control Number 2009927793

Printed in China

9 8 7 6 5 4 3 2 1